THE WITCH

ɛ⁄ɔ

A PLAY BY
CHARLES WILLIAMS

ɛ⁄ɔ

British Library Cataloguing-in-Publication Data
A catalogue record for this book is available from
the British Library

A HISTORY OF THE THEATRE

'The Theatre' is a collaborative form of fine art that uses live performers to present the experience of a real or imagined event. The performers may communicate this experience to the audience through combinations of gesture, speech, song, music, and dance, with elements of art, stagecraft and set design used to enhance the physicality, presence and immediacy of the experience. The specific place of the performance is also named by the word 'theatre' – derived from the Ancient Greek word *théatron*, meaning 'a place for viewing', itself from *theáomai*, meaning 'to see', 'watch' or 'observe'.

Modern Western theatre largely derives from ancient Greek drama, from which it borrows technical terminology, classification into genres, and many of its themes, stock characters, and plot elements. The city-state of Athens is where 'theatre' as we know it originated, as part of a broader culture of theatricality and performance in classical Greece that included festivals, religious rituals, politics, law, athletics, music, poetry, weddings, funerals, and symposia. Participation in the city-state's many festivals – and attendance at the City Dionysia as an audience member (or even as a participant in the theatrical productions) in particular, was an important part of citizenship.

The theatre of ancient Greece consisted of three types of drama: tragedy, comedy, and the satyr play (a form of tragicomedy, similar in spirit to the bawdy satire of burlesque). The origins of theatre in ancient Greece, according to Aristotle (384–322 BCE), the first theoretician of theatre, are to be found in the festivals that honoured Dionysus. These performances (the aforementioned City Dionysia) were held in semi-circular auditoria cut into hillsides, capable of seating 10,000–20,000 people. The stage consisted of a dancing floor (orchestra), dressing room and scene-building area (skene). Since the words were the most important part, good acoustics and clear delivery were paramount. The actors (always men) wore masks appropriate to the characters they represented, and each might play several parts.

Athenian tragedy (the oldest surviving form of tragedy) emerged sometime during the sixth century BCE, and flowered during the fifth century BCE – from the end of which it began to spread throughout the Greek world – and continued in popularity until the beginning of the Hellenistic period. Aeschylus, Sophocles, and Euripides were masters of the genre. The other side of the coin – Athenian comedy, is conventionally divided into three periods; 'Old Comedy', 'Middle Comedy', and 'New Comedy'. Old Comedy survives today largely in the form of the eleven surviving plays of Aristophanes, while Middle Comedy is largely lost (preserved only in a few relatively short fragments in authors such as Athenaeus of Naucratis). New Comedy is known primarily from the substantial papyrus fragments of Menander.

Western theatre developed and expanded considerably under the Romans. The theatre of ancient Rome was a thriving and diverse art form, ranging from festival performances of street theatre, nude dancing, and acrobatics, to the staging of Plautus's broadly appealing situation comedies, to the high-style, verbally elaborate tragedies of Seneca. Although Rome had a native tradition of performance, the Hellenization of Roman culture in the third century BCE had a profound and energizing effect on Roman theatre and encouraged the development of Latin literature of the highest quality for the stage. This tradition fed into the modern theatre we know today, and during the renaissance, theatre generally moved away from the poetic drama of the Greeks, and towards a more naturalistic prose style of dialogue. By the nineteenth century and the Industrial Revolution, this trend continued to progress.

In England, theatre was immensely popular, but took a big pause during 1642 and 1660 because of Cromwell's Interregnum. Prior to this, 'English renaissance theatre' was witnessed, with celebrated playwrights such as William Shakespeare, Christopher Marlowe and Ben Jonson. Under Queen Elizabeth, drama was a unified expression as far as social class was concerned, and the Court watched the same plays the commoners saw in the public playhouses. With the development of the private theatres, drama became more oriented towards the tastes and values of an upper-class audience however. By the later part of the reign of Charles I, few new plays were being written for the public theatres, which sustained themselves on the accumulated works of the previous decades. Theatre was now seen as something sinful and the Puritans tried very hard to drive it out of their society. Due to this stagnant period, once Charles II came back to the throne in 1660, theatre (among other arts) exploded with influences from France, and the wider continent.

The eighteenth century saw the widespread introduction of women to the stage – a development previously unthinkable. These women were looked at as celebrities (also a newer concept, thanks to ideas on individualism that were beginning to be born in Renaissance Humanism) but on the other hand, it was still very new and revolutionary. Comedies were full of the young and very much in vogue, with the storyline following their love lives: commonly a young roguish hero professing his love to the chaste and free minded heroine near the end of the play, much like Sheridan's *The School for Scandal*. Many of the comedies were fashioned after the French tradition, mainly Molière (the great comedic playwright), again harking back to the French influence of the King and his court after their exile.

After this point, there was an explosion of theatrical styles. Throughout the nineteenth century, the popular theatrical forms of Romanticism, melodrama, Victorian burlesque and the well-made plays of Scribe and Sardou gave way to the problem plays of Naturalism and Realism; the farces of Feydeau; Wagner's operatic *Gesamtkunstwerk*; musical theatre (including Gilbert and Sullivan's operas); F. C. Burnand's, W. S. Gilbert's and Wilde's drawing-room comedies; Symbolism; proto-Expressionism in the late works of August Strindberg and Henrik Ibsen; and Edwardian musical comedy. The list continues! These trends continued through the twentieth century in the realism of Stanislavski and Lee Strasberg, the political theatre of Erwin Piscator and Bertolt Brecht, the so-called Theatre of the Absurd of Samuel Beckett and Eugène Ionesco, and the rise of American and British musicals.

Theatre itself has an incredibly long history, and despite the massive proliferation of theatrical styles and mediums – it essentially owes its existence to the ancient Greeks and the Romans. The three main genres; tragedy, comedy and satyre, continue to influence plot themes, directing, writing and acting, with frequent and fascinating interrelations and overlaps. As a genre, it remains as popular today as it has ever been, and continues as a massive influence on popular culture more broadly. It is hoped that the current reader enjoys this book on the subject.

CHARLES WILLIAMS

Charles Walter Stansby Williams was born in London in 1886. He dropped out of University College London in 1904, and was hired by Oxford University Press as a proof-reader, quickly rising to the position of editor. While there, arguably his greatest editorial achievement was the publication of the first major English-language edition of the works of the Danish philosopher Søren Kierkegaard.

Williams began writing in the twenties and went on to publish seven novels. Of these, the best-known are probably *War in Heaven* (1930), *Descent into Hell* (1937), and *All Hallows' Eve* (1945) – all fantasies set in the contemporary world. He also published a vast body of well-received scholarship, including a study of Dante entitled *The Figure of Beatrice* (1944) which remains a standard reference text for academics today, and a highly unconventional history of the church, *Descent of the Dove* (1939). Williams garnered a number of well-known admirers, including T. S. Eliot, W. H. Auden and C. S. Lewis. Towards the end of his life, he gave lectures at Oxford University on John Milton, and received an honorary MA degree. Williams died almost exactly at the close of World War II, aged 58.

In exitu Israel

TALIESSIN'S SONG OF LOGRES

Logres lieth with sorrow riven—
  how shall the lord of salvation come?—
to the wolves, the pagans, the pirates given,
  to the hordes and the galleys of heathendom.
From the rocky hills and the roaring sea
the kings come down and our people flee.
  When shall the lord of salvation draw
armies after him? till we know
  peace that springeth from tables of law,
Logres waileth in desolate woe.

Uther Pendragon is king no more;
  lieth he deep in a royal tomb.
O but the robbers from shore to shore
  ride and ravage and sit in his room.
As wind, as thunder, as fire, they go;
Logres waileth in desolate woe.
  They ride in the place of a throne unmade,
they roar and crash in a shaken sky
  as the planets roared ere their path was stayed,
and the world was ordered, in peace to fly.

All the fierceness that ruled of yore
  is come again upon Logres strand,
King Brandegoris of Strangore,
  King Clariance of Northumberland;
King Urience over his plunder smiles;
King Lot of Orkney and all the isles
  hath sworn a league with King Agwisaunce
to send their ships on the little ports;
  on the inland towns with an evil lance
King Idras rides from his southern forts.

B

The nameless king of the hundred knights
    hath burned the castle of Terrabil;
King Cradlemas worketh his bloody rites
    in the city of Camelot at his will;
no word from Byzantion is come,
where the Emperor sitteth blind and dumb;
    in his hall of Benwick the good King Ban
is shut by Duke Cambenet's tyranny;
    from Brittany King Leodogran
dare not adventure over sea.

The wolves run wild in the snowy woods,
    as the hounds of Satan they run and howl;
no man hath surety of life or goods
    nor maiden safety, but all goes foul;
and the Roman sits in Byzantion,
no help comes down from the Sacred Throne,
    but the lords of chaos go roaring by,
and creation ruins where'er they go,
    order is lost in earth and sky,
Logres lieth in desolate woe.

Loosed are the powers of earth and air,
    fire and water in combat leap;
space is now but a broken stair,
    and the great sun runs on the edge of a steep
dizzy with terror; for all around
the elementals again abound
    in clamour and freedom; water, fire,
earth and air unprison their powers,
    and no prayer reacheth the heavenly Sire
where he sitteth calm in his lucid towers.

Myriad atoms of man and beast
  strive apart as the kingdom strives;
within and without hath concord ceased
  for terror striketh the least of lives;
the summer gnat in his flight upsprings
for rage of the torment that takes his wings,
  the wolves for hunger but more for pain
howl and ravin about the moors,
  chaos is come upon earth again
and the pirates drive upon Logres' shores.

Dubric the Shepherd lieth hid
  in cellars of Cantuar and its towns,
Winchester keepeth its Bishop amid
  huts and copses of southward downs;
but I will go, as one goeth far
to the saint that sits by the morning star,
  over the sea and the land of Gaul
to the house of the Emperor's majesty
  to view if such evil there befall
or whether some help upon earth may be.

The popes and patriarchs watch with him,
  sitting around him on golden thrones,
studying sayings of cherubim
  or adepts ranked in celestial zones;
there in a mitre and woven robe
sitteth the Master of all the globe—
  consuls and tribunes before his feet
bear their part in the rule of man,
  and the camel-drivers in the street
unload the tribute of Ispahan.

TALIESSIN'S SONG OF LOGRES

I, Taliessin, a goddess' son,
    nurtured the round Welsh hills among,
who also have not unwisely done
    in courts of music and schools of song,
I will take ship for the Sacred Throne
and there will I make one verse alone,
    one lament for the world that falls,
one cry for help ere the worst is done,
    I will send it shrill through the Emperor's halls:
This will I do in Byzantion.

For Logres is fallen, is fallen at last
    into a doom no heart can stay,
now champion and warrior flee aghast,
    no prefect rides up the Roman way.
Uther is dead, Pendragon is dead,
the soul of man is a leaf that is shed
    on storms of winter; I hear its wail
perish in darkness, wherefore I go
    to see if lordship can still prevail.
Logres lieth in desolate woe.

THE WITCH

The action takes place in a village of the West country some time early in the nineteenth century. The scene is outside a ruinous cottage on the edge of a common: a neglected road runs before it; beyond is the open country.

ACT I

[Evening. ANNE comes in.]

ANNE [knocking]: Bess! Bess! art there? 'tis I, 'tis Anne
    that calls.
BESS [at the door]: None other, I warrant me; none other
    comes
to see the outcast, the old crone, the witch.
ANNE: Fair fall them then and you! Good cheer, old
    Bess;
here is butter, here are eggs, my husband bade
bring hither when time served the walk.
BESS: For this
your sow shall run unharmed this breeding time.
ANNE: That's as may be; our thanks for the goodwill.
BESS: There's no goodwill in me nor in the folk
that point thumbs after me behind a hedge;
aye, and curse under breath and then aloud
when all their curses do not save their hens
from laying addled eggs or none at all.
ANNE: God a mercy, Bess, and would you curse their hens
because a dozen women cackle more
than all the hens God's mercy ever made?
Who cares for what a flock of hens can do,
perching and perking and scrabbling in the dirt?
BESS: Why, so—to see them flap and scurry aside
and all in a flurry drive their chickens home
when I go peeping by the lane's corner.
ANNE: Chut!
You like to see them run?
BESS: And others than they
skirr when the witch looks out of doors at the world.
ANNE: What pleasure to see men's faces fall awry,

or such a girl's heart as your Rhoda's beat
with fear of her sweetheart dying from no pain
but that same lingering fever in his breast
as melting wax—to those that dread it—brings?
BESS: Ah Anne, well-to-do Anne, farm-owning Anne,
    you have not lain abed December nights,
    cold more than needs for but one blanket's need,
    snow in the chimney, and no food to hand,
    yet warm as a fox in his burrow just to know
    that some strong man, some man much like your Giles,
    lay shivering all the night, with blankets enow
    to keep his feet warm, but no warmth at heart,
    for just a little snick of fear within,
    lest you should hate him—
ANNE: Giles would never fear!—
BESS: or his wife or babies, comfortable Anne.
    And there's a rich man too, there's the squire's self,
    'twixt fear and anger sleeps but little of nights.
    That keeps me warmer than the great log fire
    piled in his hall when first October blows.
ANNE: But what's your gain, Bess, if they fear you so?
BESS: Just to lie there and know a poor old crone,
    with her rheumatic finger on their throats,
    fingers their windpipes; so they draw deep breaths,
    cursing her curses, but they doze with dreams . . .
    Anne, have you ever watched your Giles asleep?
ANNE: God a mercy, Bess, I sleep as sound as he;
    no time to sit and watch him in the day,
    less time to lie and watch him in the night.
    Besides, all's under God.
BESS: Aye, and strange things
    go running abroad in the moonlight under him.

He has watched a million moons out, and not stooped
. to check one weaselly red-bellied shape,
   that might be vermin and might be something else,
   loosed from a witch's door when clocks strike twelve.
ANNE: It's living alone and looking at the moon
   that makes you think so. Rhoda's just a girl.
Come over this winter and share a room with us,
I'll warrant you see no vermin.
BESS: And be warm,
   and fed, and cossetted—and not a smile
   to be struck off a face when I come in,
   but the squire to give me cloth and take the land.
   If I was out, he'd quick enough be in—
   this strip that parts him from the common land
   and keeps his wall from going where it will.
   Fine straying walls squires have, like straying mares,
   to go all over the world and come back home,
   when they have eaten their fill of others' grass.
   I block him here, and bitter he finds it too.
   Black witchcraft isn't only in the poor.
ANNE: There's few that say so. How does your Rhoda
     keep?
BESS: O finely, finely, going about the world.
   She's got her longing, and shall find it out.
   I know.
ANNE: And will you help to give it her?
BESS: There's something here in me that rules the world
   from dawn to sunset; farm and village and town
   lurk watching for it, and when once it comes
   it helps them out to get what they desire.
   Witchcraft or devilry or fate: there's craft
   to rule the lazy kingdoms of the world

or get a child the heart of her desire,
and I will get it her, before the years
have puzzled men three times with hate and fear.
ANNE: Bess, don't you think too much of hate and fear
  and hunger? Hunger never filled itself,
  and odd things come with thinking of odd things.
BESS: It's no odd thing she needs. Look.
ANNE: What, she walks
  with the squire's agent then?
BESS: None such for her;
  I sang a catch with a black-horned goat one night
  to see what he would tell me, and he sang—
  Youth, riches, knighthood—a thrice-tangled tale.
ANNE: Well, I don't love Ralph Carter near enough
  to stop and meet him.
BESS: Fear him then, wise Anne?
ANNE: Fear him? I fear him? there's no rent been owed,
  quarter by quarter, since we held the farm.
  I'd fear you sooner.
BESS: Wisely said; your sow
  shall surely run unharmed and get its young,
  nor shall Giles break his leg when mending roofs.
  Husband and sow safe, will you long for more?
[ANNE goes out with something like a snort, as RALPH CARTER and
                    RHODA come in]
RHODA: Mother, here's Mr. Carter, with a word
  to say to you yourself.
BESS: A word for me?
  Bless us, a word—vixen or harridan,
  old bitch—that's two; one from the squire, and one
  from Mr. Carter's sweet good-languaged self.
  He hasn't got his master's tongue—nor I

an ear to hear a serving-man's abuse,
save what a flick to my little Malkin boy
may set him on to answer. Malkin's the lad
to steal by night and suck fat servants' blood;
ease them, and save them physic. Well, the word?
CARTER: Ha, ha! Why, old Bess, you've a proper tongue
to tease the squire's friends.—Don't go, Rhoda.
BESS: No,
Rhoda; don't go; the squire's man bids you stay.
Curtsey to thank him. If you were a lady, child,
and had a footman for your coach, d'you think
he'd be too plump and lazy?
CARTER: Look you, Bess,
I give you license—
BESS: Step inside, and see
if there's a rabbit hanging in the smoke,
trapped ... trapped ... trapped ... so.
CARTER: You don't snare rabbits, Bess.
BESS: No? I've got something trapped hanging inside;
the squire's pet thought—a bouncing baby, trapped.
Wishes grow fat, and when they can't grow deeds,
the old witch keeps them dangling in her shed.
It's growing plump with longing now, that wish
the squire bred in his brain for me to snare.
Wishes go bad when they've been kept too long.
RHODA: Let's hear him, mother.
CARTER: Rhoda, you're a lass
that knows where profit lies.
BESS: Not yet, not quite.
It takes more talk than Rhoda's ever had
by nights with little Malkin, or his sire,
my master, the tall black who sent him here.

CARTER: Rhoda, I told you I'd a word to say
  that might do good to all. This hut's too old
  for any Christian soul. Now up the hill
  there's a new cottage with two rooms. The squire
  offers your mother this in change for hers.
BESS: And the land this stands on?
CARTER: Ten pounds for the land;
  ten pounds, and a cottage twice as good as this.
BESS: And then the squire's wall could go straying out
  just where his ugly nightmare runs each night,
  and graze on the common. Should I sleep so warm?
CARTER: Warm?
BESS: Aye, with joy to know the squire can't sleep.
  O aye, I've got his baby hanging up,
  his wish, his wish. And if he had this hut,
  he'd get his precious baby back again.
  It goes with the hut, my clever serving-man.
RHODA: Mother—
BESS: Be quiet, child.
CARTER: Aye, be quiet, child. Bess,
  it's well to hush her. She might wish for room
  to stretch an arm in and not strike the wall
  unless the broken window let it through.
  Rhoda, I thought of you the whole long while
  I quarrelled with the squire to make the change.
  And here's your mother quarrelling with you,
  only for fear that you might want the change.
  Well, take it as you will. I meant my best.
BESS: Rhoda's your best? better than all your best,
  and meat for your betters, serving-man. Go back
  and tell your master I'm too old to lose
  the land and the hut and the baby in the smoke;

the baby that gets fat as he gets lean.

CARTER: Rhoda?

BESS: No word.

RHODA: Mother—

BESS: No word. I know
what Malkin means to come, and what I mean.

CARTER: What's Malkin then to keep you here?

BESS: My chuck,
my sweet boy, my dear imp, my little black
bad-hearted agile fancy; he that sits
couched on my shoulder or my knee, and sings
of what he runs about the world to do,
drop sparks, lame cows, or whisper in the ear
of squires nigh sick for walls that can't get out
over the common. Little Malkin sweet!

CARTER: If you should talk so to a justice, witch—

BESS: Isn't the squire a justice?

CARTER: If he heard
Bedlam might take you, and the whips and chains
kept for such maniacs as believe they talk
with such an imp of the devil under the moon.

RHODA: Ah!

CARTER: Nay, forgive me, child; it is her way.
What pleasure she finds in it I cannot tell
and would not grudge her, but to keep you close
in this half-hut, half-sty—that maddens me.
Forgive me; I must needs be jealous for you
who are too mild to be so for yourself.
Here's the squire coming.

BESS: Squire and justice too,
and cock o' the village on all hearths but here.

[The SQUIRE comes in]

CARTER [to him]: I've told her; she won't bite. Try if it tastes
sweeter from yours the master's hand, than mine.
SQUIRE: Well, Bess, have you heard my offer? Come, be wise.
Think on your children.
BESS: Ah that's what I do,
evening and morning. Would they prosper, squire—
or would she prosper that's the only one
left here to tell me what love meant? They say
she favours her father—a fine figure, squire.
SQUIRE: Yes, it's a hard thing to be left alone.
BESS: Don't we both know it? Why, your lady, squire,
she would have been now just my husband's age.
SQUIRE: Not by a score of years; and see you, Bess,
don't lick my wife's name with your tongue.
BESS: Why, no.
She *was* a lady, wasn't she? Not like
farm-maids or witches or women of the town.
SQUIRE: Keep your mouth shut.
CARTER: Gently, go gently, sir,
or she'll refuse you just to thwart your will.
BESS: Why now, what harm in a gay lady's life?
'Tisn't for us who are moral, being poor—
Rhoda and me: *her* honesty's her trade;
but you and your boy I warrant have known a mort
of women to drink with and slip bodices down.
Isn't a college town a likely place
for come-by-nights to play in?
SQUIRE: God's my life!
You—get out, Carter!—you black beldame! you!
you'd foul my son's name? you'd twitch tales of him?

where's your own? hanged in London now belike,
as you shall be—or burned for witchcraft!

BESS: Me
for witchcraft? there was a jovial squire once burned
a witch for her craft—she was a witch with power—
and on the year's mind of her death it fell
his son was borne to Bedlam, and his goods
and lands all went to ruin for want of an heir.
Witches don't only work while they're alive;
but leave the spiders in the manor house
to sit by a young heir's pillow and spin him dreams
out of their bellies, till his brain's no more
than a fat spider's belly of sticky web.

SQUIRE: God curse you!

BESS: Ah God's like to listen to you;
He never listens to a wish; that's why
all who wish strongly have to slip and find
the black man who sends Malkin. Farewell, squire.
Go back to your gay London dame my son
whistled in London, ere she liked your gold.

                      [She goes into the hut

CARTER [leaving RHODA, with whom he has been whisper-
     ing from time to time]: You've lost her?

SQUIRE: Damn her, she'll lose home and life.
I'll draw a warrant—

CARTER: Better not.

SQUIRE: Why not?
I tell you she shan't bully me for naught.
She'll rue it.

CARTER: Better not.

SQUIRE: Why, you don't think
there's anything in her talk?

CARTER: I think wise men
don't put out poison on the supper board
when their sons come from Oxford. Go you home
and quiet yourself to meet him there. I'll come
after a word with the girl.

SQUIRE: I won't believe
in all this devil's work—God keep us safe!
why don't the village try her in the pond
or stone her all at once with none to blame?

CARTER: And that may come, but keep you far enough.
Get back, or Gerald will be home ere you,
and pacing up and down the terrace stones
and quoting poetry softly to himself,
quite out of heart with you and all you want
to talk of with him; yes, and you must needs
go softly with your visitor at the house.

SQUIRE: That's not his business.

CARTER: Lest he make it so,
be early there to talk with him. See you,
I know your son—he's all in love with words;
anything's right so long as it's finely said.

SQUIRE: I can't talk finely.

CARTER: Talk to him of yourself;
he'll make the fineness. Why, the commonest maid
talking to him in twilight here would touch
his young heart into ecstasy, and her words
make of his ear a tiring room to come
thence like play-acting queens into his brain.
Be quiet, be simple. Get you home to him.
I'll follow.

SQUIRE: Carter, if she died the house—

CARTER: 'Tchut. If she died, the house would drop apart

with wind and rain. Leave it at that.

SQUIRE: You'll come?

CARTER: At once. No warrants till I've tried the girl.

                              [The SQUIRE goes out

Kiss me; it's dark enough.   [RHODA kisses him

Why I stay here!— and why you make me stay!—

Fine buffers for two lunatics to bruise!

The squire's least mad, he's crazy for the land,

but what your mother's crazy for none knows.

RHODA: That's where she's strong; I think none knows
    her will;

perhaps she has no will except her will.

Ralph, I could once have been as strong as she

if . . .

CARTER: If?

RHODA: Don't make me say it.

CARTER: No excuse;

out with it.

RHODA: If you—isn't that enough?

The witch's daughter to be just a girl

because a man is stronger!

CARTER: Ah that's it,

isn't it, Rhoda?

RHODA: If my mother knew!

BESS [from the hut]: Rhoda!

CARTER: She doesn't. Come away with me.

Why must we stay?

RHODA: I know . . . but, Ralph, to feel

myself in London and no guard but you;

no rock but you to build on! It's too sweet,

too terrible with sweetness; let me taste

a little longer.

                    c

CARTER: What, still frightened?

RHODA: Just
  to look at being frightened—

BESS: Rhoda!

RHODA: Hark,
  I can't stay now. Besides, Ralph, you've known girls—
  you know they like to feel themselves pressed on,
  still holding fast: but once let go, one arm
  only to cling to—that's a different joy.
  I wouldn't change this joy for that too soon.

CARTER: Whimsies! If you'd known men as I've known
    girls
  you'd know the pleasure was in being loved,
  not thinking about it.

RHODA: If I'd been the first!

CARTER: The first or one-and-twentieth, all's the same.
  I bet you've kissed a farm-hand—every way,
  for all I care; I don't begrudge it. Love's
  as fresh as ever if the heart's as good
  and the will in it.

BESS: Rhoda!

RHODA: I must go;
  good-night. She's coming. Good-night; go. Good-
    night.
          [He kisses her and goes. BESS comes from the hut.]
  Did you want me, mother?

BESS: Naught but to stay here.
  One's coming worth our pains.

RHODA: Who? the squire's son?

BESS: Stay so, and bless the moon for shining out.
  He'll come this way.

RHODA: Why must I talk to him?

BESS: Because the moon and you and clever talk
  will maze what brains he's got, and then he's yours.
  You'll waste time with the servant; here's the heir.
RHODA: He won't dare wed me!
BESS: Wait till his father knows.
  I've watched them years; a pretty boy; he went
  dreaming, and dreams still. Oxford's near by night,
  and Malkin knows him or I know him there.
  Show him his dreams; talk little but talk well.
RHODA: But what do we catch if we should catch the heir?
BESS: I'd go to hell to see the squire gone dazed
  to know the witch's daughter got with child—
  or let him think so; there are herbs to turn
  seed into barrenness. And then the gold
  he'll offer and we'll spill! O Rhoda girl,
  the game's beginning. Hark, he's coming; back
  a little into the hut; then out, and wait.
                          [They move into the hut door
GERALD [without]: Good-night; good-night. 'A fair
  good-night to all.'   [He comes in
Well rid of you, good fellows! I have dreamed
a thousand years in this half-hour, and felt
the clouds quench all the catches. This is night,
being the solitude wherein the mind
considers its own beauty, dark and full
and far from the rough noises of the world,
so that a friend's voice is intrusion; yes,
not even the sacred poets yet have found
a name for the only voice that Silence owns—
unless that god the Mediterranean drowned
were it, unless our master Shelley were it,
marvellous, aboriginal, divine.

If such a voice should sound now, if this night
and silence and the whole invisible mind
of the dark universe should speak some word
simple as its own nature; it might be,
if deafness did not clog our mortal ears.

BESS [at the door to RHODA]: All's yours now; speak to
    him. He's yet too young
to know if speech like yours be false or true.
He hears the voice and not the accent—go.

RHODA: Sir, did you want my mother?

GERALD: I?

RHODA: I thought
you looked . . . forgive me.

GERALD: This is more than chance;
this is the longing of all loveliness
to find a voice. Who is your mother, child?

RHODA: She lives here, in this hut. I thought you came
to find her.

GERALD: Child, your mother was the moon
immaculately conceiving in some dark
valley of Latmos the inconceivable
Beauty's most holy incarnation. Say,
have you not heard—has not a rumour spread
you are the very daughter of the moon?

RHODA: O not the moon, but one that knows the moon.
I am the child of a wise woman, born,
certainly, when the moon was very high
on a March evening.

GERALD: No—you are the Spring,
you are Persephone, maiden and queen,
at the winter solstice turning from the dark.
Stand still, and let me play with dreams of you.

I will not hear your name.

RHODA: Perhaps indeed
I have no true name, for my mother says
our true names are enchantment and not known,
or if known never to be sounded forth
among the uninstructed.

GERALD: O wise maid,
I have spent years in Oxford but to taste
antique philosophies springing from that root.
Will you be found as wise as Oxford seems?

RHODA: I have no wisdom, but my mother says
no man can utterly have power on us
unless he call us by our hidden names.

GERALD: Tell me your name then; tell me your hidden
name.

RHODA: Why, would you utterly have power on me?

GERALD: I would have power on you or you on me.
It is a perilous thing to meet by night
upon these heaths a more than mortal maid
and talk with her, unless there is a strength
to pass unhurt and leave her. No mere song
brought Orpheus past the Sirens, but their names
cried o'er the ocean drew them to their doom;
it was the strife of Pan to speak the name
of our Chief Master that made black the sun,
and when the god's mouth failed upon the large
syllables of that Tetragrammaton,
all nature moaned, crying that Pan was dead.
And I would bind you, whether you be maid,
fairy, or goddess, or what other shape
of fabulous imagination now
my mind mistakes you for, with such iron spells

as the adepts once in Eleusis knew
to prop the portcullis of the underworld.
RHODA: Whether I were a goddess or a maid
you should not hold me but by other bands.
GERALD: O but the stronger hold the weaker bands;
Cynthia, consider all things are within,
nor think that when you, with a holy kiss,
first wooed your brother, chaste Endymion,
into the clear virginity of love,
his sleep knew other than your very self
breathed over him in your significant name.
RHODA: I do not know these names.
GERALD: They are your past,
but you are willing to forget them now.
And be content to lose them. Do you know
that he you speak to is a mortal man,
or do you dream that you are still afar
among the immortal gods in Thessaly?
RHODA: I know the farmers and the farmers' boys,
but beyond these I know my mother tells
of other meetings where the tribe of the air
mingle at midnight with such human folk
as ride upon strange horses to the feast.
GERALD: What is your mother?
RHODA: A wise woman.
GERALD: Wise
indeed if she can know the ancient things;
and what are you? Tell me your worldly name.
RHODA: My name is Rhoda—
GERALD: Ay, I had forgot.
You are the daughter of old Bess the witch—
RHODA: Will you too speak of her as farmers do?

GERALD: You have forgotten me; you never saw
  a boy look at you from behind a hedge
  as boys will at such beauty as they feel
  bears them into a rapture out of time.
  I know you, Rhoda; when I was a boy,
  being forbidden to pass by this way
  lest your wise mother should put spells on me,
  I stopped here once and saw you.
RHODA: At that hour
  I think you came for ever to my dreams,
  but then I never dreamed that you would make
  a jest of me, as all this while you do.
GERALD: I jest?
RHODA: Call me a goddess, fairy-born,
  moon-nurtured. You have shamed me.
GERALD: Never that.
  Being mortal, you are even more divine
  than if you were mere goddess. O your hand
  has meaning in it more than deities have
  when they unclothe their being of its cloud.
  Rhoda, it is not I can scorn or shame;
  do not forget me, do not go from me.
RHODA: You are the squire's son, and I am the child
  of a wise woman; loose me, let me go.
GERALD: Your face is like the Oxford halls by night
  seen from some neighbouring hill where poets dwell,
  or like a page of Hebrew charms—so full
  are they of meaning; were you all they meant?
RHODA: Leave me, I cannot bear it, let me dream.
GERALD: No dreaming—all significant and full
  of purpose. Rhoda, can the squire's son dare
  hold these hands fast? these that have made the world,

and are the origin of space and time?
Sweet, can I let you go?
RHODA: You must, you must;
I am not meant for you—I—O let go;
To-morrow, if you will.
GERALD: To-morrow? no,
this is to-morrow; only in your eyes
the future sits—if I should part from you
I should go out of the universe; God made
nothing but you, and outside you and Him
there is eternal nothingness and void.
RHODA: But I—you said—am a wise woman's child
and know there is to-morrow. Let me go;
come if you will and see my face by day,
and then perhaps you will not grieve to know
I and to-morrow need no more be one.
GERALD: A challenge?
RHODA: Yes, a challenge—go your way.
A challenge—till to-morrow.
GERALD: Undo then
this spell with other spells. [He kisses her.] No challenge; naught
but the most inward silence of the night.
[He looks at her and goes. When he is out of hearing RHODA turns
to her mother]
RHODA: I think he'll come to-morrow.
BESS [from the door]: O he'll come.
I have a way of knowing; keep your talk
simple and innocent and yet sounding wise.
But he'll believe you wise, whether or no,
being drunk with youth and beauty and his dreams.
RHODA: And when he comes?

BESS: I find a way to pull
the squire to ruin or you to the squire's chair,
and either way the squire will fret to death,
and round his bed will my black lord and I
foot a gay ghostly dance that he shall see
but not the doctor nor the maids. O rare!
If you shall know him sick and see me squat
very still in the embers, do not touch
my shoulder—no more than on Sabbath nights—
I shall be dancing in the squire's great room.
O! O! come, Malkin! O Malkin, little chuck,
won't you sit mewing on the window ledge,
and grin at squire's eyes? Sick, O sick to death,
and what a brave dance shall we singing three
beat out his breath with! Come, girl.
RHODA: Yes, but I?
What will you give me if I give myself
to all this toilsomeness of being loved?
BESS: The boy for a husband or a hundred pounds:
And I and the wise devil for your friends.
Come in.

> [She begins singing

        Hey, when I saw a man in red
        then I knew that I was dead;
        he had a crownet on his head,
            and he smiled awry at me;
        smiled awry and gave me a kiss,
        and a black pinch somewhere I-wis,
            and we danced blithe and free.

            [The second stanza is heard from within the hut
        Hey, when I saw the black man grow
        and never a shadow did he throw;

the moon shone bright, and all below
 the corpses laughed at me;
 hooves and feet went quickly then,
 and I danced an hour with two dead men,
 and we danced blithe and free.

ACT II

[A week later. Morning. DAN comes in hastily and raps fiercely
at the shut door]

DAN: Hey, hey! Hey, mother! Rhoda! who's astir?
 Hey there! God strike them! Mother! Rhoda! Wake!
BESS [within]: Who's there? who hunts the witch so
 early? [Opening] Dan?
DAN: Dan right enough! No one's been here for me?
 No asking what I am or where? no dogs
 snuffling the door-planks?
BESS: Dogs!
DAN: Men then; no men
 with horses, sticks, and pistols?
BESS: Bow Street men!
 Dan, are the runners out for you?
DAN: This week.
 It's taken me more than that to get down here
 from London by side-roads. You haven't heard?
 Nor Rhoda? Rhoda hears more tales than you.
BESS: You're shaking.
DAN: I shall shake at the end of a rope
 if they get hands on me. There's a dead man
 up there in Houndsditch, and a live man here.
BESS: Gold or a doxy or just pretty hate?
DAN: Hate first, then gold. A good thing hate got pleased

or I'd no profit at all from killing him—
the gold went to get free; thief-takers' charge
for an hour's start of the runners.

BESS: Ay; and now—
the wood's your place, the pit by the hollow tree.

DAN: For how long, Mother? I can't muffle there
till old squire dies and justices forget.
No, I'm for Bristol.

BESS: There's no money here
to help you to a passage.

DAN: No? that's strange.
Mother, I never knew a woman yet—
not the most spendthrift hussy, nor the worst
overworked maid of any London lord,
nor country harridan (not meaning you)—
who couldn't find a sixpence at a pinch.
Find sixpence, Mother.

BESS: Ah, the pretty boy.
Comes wanting his old mother's stocking. Dan,
you'd kill me for it, wouldn't you?

DAN: Why no.
You'll give it me. Food first and then the gold.

BESS: You're like the rest. If I had any store,
where do you think my pleasure would be gone,
in frightening all the safe-saved farmers' grins?
I should be one of them. I shouldn't know
there isn't a thing in all the world I have
except this half-roof and the curse that goes
about the village as fire about a barn.
When the squire threw me a shilling six months since
I threw it back to him, for fear it broke
the utter poverty that makes me rich.

DAN: Well, food first. If you'd come along by night
  you'd need it—or is food as scant as gold?

BESS: An egg and a crust or two; kind souls that bring
  presents, to keep on the windward side the witch.

           [RHODA comes in from the country]

DAN: Hey, Rhoda!

RHODA: Dan!

DAN: Listen, a kiss for me,
  and a penny to save my legs down Bristol way.

RHODA: Ask Mother.

DAN: I've asked Mother!

RHODA: Ask her then
  what fathers pay to get their children born.

DAN: Fathers?

BESS: Slip snare! slip snare! the rabbit's in!
  Weasel, you've caught him?

RHODA: Or he me.

BESS: Trash, trash!
  I blow them into ruin with a breath!
  O the squire's wish! O rare girl! O his boy
  trammelled before the world's grin!

RHODA: Do we grin?
  Suppose the village hate me more than him?

BESS: O well done, Malkin! O rare girl, well done!
  Did he need squeezing?

DAN: What's this, then?

BESS: Go in;
  I'll brew the herbs to-night; a torn sheet serves
  to frighten them, if he should last as long.
  No, Rhoda, stop. Get down to the village now—
  you've been asleep, I warrant—go to Anne,
  Giles' wife, and bid her come; beg her to come.

Be shy, be shamefaced, wench. Anne's a good heart,
and a power in all the farms; she pities you.
Good heart, be glad to stand by love-lost girls.
Chuck Malkin, work! O a fat meal for this.

DAN: Are you both mad?

BESS: Gold for you too, boy Dan.

RHODA [stopping as she goes]: Never this toil for him to
    spend on dice—
Mother, no gold for that.

DAN: A pretty girl!
Will have me hanged first ere she lends me gold.

RHODA: No chance of that.

DAN: Much chance of that, my lass,
if Bow Street runners come to find me here.

RHODA: Shake your own heels then, lest they shake in
    air,
over the hills to Bristol; there's the road.

DAN: And there's the road from London, whence the dogs
come scouring for me. If you go that way—
I'd as lief kill twice as once, being hanged but once.

RHODA: Ay, you would kill and make no profit. Pah!
Dan, you're the foolishest creature in the shire.
You never look for profit anyway,
luck-wasting spender.

DAN: Keep a tighter tongue.
You always saw and sneaked your profit out,
like a kerchief-miker, never ran a game
for no thought but the glory.

BESS: Ah, young blood!
There, there, sweet babes; we've no time now for
    this.
Get down to Anne's; and you, boy, get inside;

there's food for need—then to the wood and hide.
Hark, there's one coming—off; both ways be gone.
[RHODA goes out; DAN into the hut. After a moment or two
TESSA enters]
TESSA [hesitating]: Am I—is this—
BESS [eyeing her]: I am the woman you want.
TESSA: Your name is Bess? I heard of you last night
and stopped my coach to find you. Are you she
who knows the future better than the past,
because you help to make it?
BESS: I am she
that knows the minds of those who seek her out.
TESSA: Your name has travelled half across the shire—
'wise woman', 'prophetess'—ten miles from here
they told me of you. I am going down
to join my husband on his Cornish lands,
but, since a peaceful heart is something gained
for two hours stoppage, turn in here to ask
what you can tell me of the years to come.
BESS: Your husband?
TESSA: You will know him by your art?
BESS: No need, if I know you. What do you need?
TESSA: Wise woman, there is sorrow in our lives
because our eldest son is overseas,
in some unknown land, and my lord is ill
so that the doctors fear his death ere spring.
BESS: I think your husband may outlast your son,
son being mere dream but husband less a dream,
for all the offices of husbandry,
leaving the name out.
TESSA: Well—you know me then?
I told the squire the game was weak enough.

BESS: I knew the squire had bought a London dame
  for some few weeks of company. You're she?
TESSA: Well guessed, wise woman. Why then do I come?
BESS: Because the squire would have a woman's eye
  judge of the pretty maid his son adores?
TESSA: Why, ay.
BESS: Or that—but this I do not think—
  the son hath begged you come and meet the maid.
TESSA: The son? O lud, wise woman! Gerald's eyes
  when first he saw me in his mother's chair—
  'Is this your friend, Sir?' 'Sir, I will not shame
  my mother's name by sitting down with her.'
  Mothers are like religion—made to ease
  youth's necessary quarrel with the old.
  So part to spite the son I came, and part
  to please the father, and to please myself
  the largest part: to see a witch at work
  and buy such cunning tricks as she might yield
  for the thanks of a few crowns, since I had thoughts
  of taking up the trade myself in town.
BESS: You, my fine lady of pleasure?
TESSA: I, my witch.
  O there are cunning women up in town
  with monstrous rooms, black dwarfs, and crystal globes,
  cost guineas, but bring guineas in as well,
  practitioners of magic.
BESS: Magic—they?
  What did you come to see?
TESSA: Why, you: what else?
  O and your daughter if she's hereabout.
  The young squire's apt to buy her, I conceive?
  Do you think she'll sell?

BESS: Do you think the squire'll buy?
[RHODA comes back with ANNE]
RHODA: Mother, here's Anne.
ANNE: What's wrong with the child, Bess?
BESS [signing to Rhoda to withdraw]: Squire,
  and squire's son. Anne, a thing's come all my craft
  never supposed. A foolish girl—but O
  Anne, was the more than folly hers or his?
  Now the wise woman seeks a wiser, now,
  will you throw back my boasting in my teeth?
  Anne, you'll be pitiful?
ANNE: But what's the . . . Bess,
  she's his?
BESS: Past all denying. O my curse
  come home!
ANNE: Poor child.
BESS: Nay, but, Anne, hark you here.
  I won't unsay a word of all I said
  of how I loathe the village, love their thumbs
  thrust out against me and the squire's black look;
  hate for hate, I dare dare them. But she's young—
  how could I know I feared for her at heart,
  as I am all in a bitter cold fear, Anne,
  unless you help her.
ANNE: Cheerly, Bess!
BESS: What cheer
  for the witch's daughter, the young squire's light o' love?
ANNE: Nay, no more one than t'other. These things chance.
  The squire'll help you.
BESS: Ah! take help from him!
  that's a wry mouthful.
ANNE: Ah, but that's your task.

BESS: Suppose he won't?

ANNE: He will.

BESS: Suppose he won't?

ANNE: The squire's hard, but he's just. Besides the whole
  stretch of his land would think shame if he failed,
  the fault being with his son. Cheerly, good Bess.

[TESSA, who has been watching the other three, seems to see some
                    one, and goes out]

BESS: The girl's too angry with herself or him
  or else too much in love to think on't yet.
  And I'm too old and hated. Anne, all's yours.
  You're a good woman. I've not thought of God
  for years, but if he's yours he must be good.

ANNE: Oh no, but we are good because he is.
  I've got to meet Giles with a message. Wait
  and I'll be back soon. We'll find things to do.

                    [She nods encouragingly and hurries off

BESS: Tell any woman she's good and give her things
  to do or manage, and she's under your thumb.
  It wags; it wags. Sweet Anne, you don't brew herbs
  to keep Giles' seed from sprouting. Hey my lass,
  remember—you've begun to think of God.
  O! O! my heart! beat gently, heart, for glee!

          [The SQUIRE bursts in, TESSA after him]

SQUIRE: What the hell's this? God blast your black lies,
    witch!
  What's this mad tale you're spreading round the world?

BESS: Rhoda, go in.

SQUIRE: Rhoda a thousand fiends!
  Stand still and face me, girl, and your grey dame!
  I'll have you flogged from here to Bristol! What,
  you dare to foul me with your spittle?

                    D

TESSA. Harry,
  be wary, or you'll make worse trouble.
  [As he turns on her] Well,
  go on. Let's hope that you'll be amusing too.
BESS: Has the young pig run grunting to his sire?
TESSA: Why no, wise woman; it was I that told,
  hearing you weeping to the farmer's wife.
  Always cheat fairly if you can. I told,
  being, after all, hired by the other side.
BESS: At least, my squire, last night's joy wasn't bought
  under the trees—as up in your great house.
SQUIRE: I'll have you cleared with convicts.
RHODA: Ay, that's fine.
  Gerald! [She cries out the name in almost a shriek
SQUIRE: If all his babble meant but this—
  If this was Plato, this was Aristotle,
  and Greek, and chatter about the moon . . . My God,
  girl, if you've made your profit from his talk—
RHODA: Fine profit! Gerald! Gerald!
SQUIRE: Damn you, stop!
  don't dare to take his name upon your lips.
RHODA [promptly and as if wildly]: Gerald!
GERALD [without]: Hallo! Rhoda? Hallo! I'm here.
  [He comes in, and goes to RHODA
  Father?
TESSA: Now, black or white? Praise God, I'm grey
  for neither black nor white is common-sense.
  I'd like it better if they sang their parts
  as they do at Covent Garden. Prompter's bell!
SQUIRE: Tessa, keep silent, damn you! Gerald, boy,
  here's a mad whisper going about the lanes
  hatched by this devil's brew in their own slime—

GERALD: Sir, I won't hear—

SQUIRE: that . . . blast it, it's not true.

GERALD: Well, sir?

SQUIRE: This girl, of all the world!

GERALD: This girl?
Sir, when you ask advisedly . . . Look up,
Rhoda; dear girl, look up. He did not speak,
you need not hear a voice again, save mine.

TESSA [to BESS]: Wise woman, you've gone silent.

BESS: Lady of love,
if you could see my Malkin! When the world's
talking so loud, we hug ourselves in peace.

SQUIRE: Look, boy, come back to the house.

GERALD: Father, you spoke
before this lady, and I answer you
before her and instead of her. What chance
brings my most duteous adoration forth
before you and your month's companion there
I shall inquire at leisure. For my heart,
I am its keeper and none other, she
alone excepted who is that heart's self.

TESSA: ⎫ ⎧O lud!
SQUIRE: ⎪ ⎪O Christ! [All at once]
BESS: ⎬ ⎨O brave!
RHODA: ⎭ ⎩O love!

GERALD: Go in, sweet. I will answer this
to him or any.

RHODA: You won't go?

GERALD: Go in,
and I will swear to see you ere I go.
No tears, princess; for I would have you weep
only for little tender loving things,

not at the grossness of the world. Go in,
be happy, since we taught each other love.
[He takes her to the hut. BESS in exquisite pleasure follows her
  Now, Sir?
SQUIRE: This is no place to talk of it . . .
  Could you find no one but my enemy?—
  This witch's baby? This—but is it true?
  No, no, for God's sake no more poetry.
  I see it's true.
GERALD: All's true as she is. Sir—
SQUIRE: You'd wed her even?
GERALD: Wed her or not wed
  is but to nod a little—more or less—
  to the degeneracy of the times.
  Marriages don't make honest women.
TESSA: No,
  but honest women make the marriages
  to see those called dishonest don't get free
  with equal pleasures and much fewer pains.
GERALD: What shall I say? Sir, if you could be glad
  that I am glad, or like me to be loved
  marvellously, by one who is a girl
  only because her deity can be known
  most perfect so; if you could wish me joy—
  such joy as God had making her—
SQUIRE: Joy? Joy?
  There's a place for your sort, fellow. You're the heir,
  are you? and spend your heirship ere it comes
  on the sweepings of the devil's kitchen, blown
  about your feet in the lanes? If there is one
  thwarts me from my just rights these many months
  it is the hag her mother, and you'll spend

all my farms' revenues on the daughter?

GERALD: Why,
if that were so—you know it is not so—
what's right in you can hardly be gross wrong
in me who am a little more than heir.
You are the presence of our House, but I
am its succession and its prophecy.
Which does the House most wrong? I keep my tongue
from more because she is a woman still.

SQUIRE: Get away; get away; get from my sight—
get into hiding lest I strike at you.
I'll burn the hut down with her in it; no,
I'll have her shipped to Tasman. O you beast—

TESSA [to GERALD]: Being a woman still, spare me the
    sight
of blood—from fight or apoplexy. Go.

          [GERALD reluctantly turns and goes into the hut
Harry, come home. You shouldn't brood so much
nor let this longing for a plot of land
grow hate of the plot's owner. Nothing's worth
so much of one mind's energy as you spend—
no, and young Gerald for the matter of that—
and even my wise witch, if all were known,
perhaps. Come home now; let us talk of it.

SQUIRE: Where's Carter?

TESSA: Lud, why Carter?

SQUIRE: I've a thought.
It came before, but then I let it slip,
and all this week it's dodged about my mind,
but Carter's wise to turn my thoughts to acts;
only it must be swift—before the news
gets round the villages.

TESSA: Well, there he is,
coming back from the big field. Call him here.
SQUIRE: No, but you call him. I can't call aloud
till something's happened. Carter will know what.
TESSA: It's strange to call across the country fields:
However—Mr. Carter!—yes, he heard—
Here!—Mr. Carter! look, he's coming down.
        [In a minute CARTER comes in]
CARTER: Good morning, Mrs. Marlow.—Squire, what's
    wrong?
SQUIRE: Tessa, go home, Don't speak. Go home, I say.
I'm coming. Straight home. Don't stand gossiping
with farmers' wives, and winking round the news.
TESSA [to CARTER]: Get him home quickly. Very well,
    Harry.   [She goes out
CARTER: What's wrong?
SQUIRE: Gerald, the cursed fool, and this young brat,
this squealing mandrake—there's what's wrong.
CARTER: What more?
The boy's been mad on her since he came down
from Oxford, and you know it.
SQUIRE: Well, he's mad
now past retrieving. I've a grandson now,
mayhap.
        [CARTER whistles]
    A grandson, Carter, a new heir.
CARTER: Gad! Damn him, he's been poaching!
SQUIRE: He's been caught.
CARTER: Umph. Well, what then?
SQUIRE: Carter, there's one way out.
Two ways—for the mother and the girl. The witch—
can't the farmhands try if she *is* a witch,

if they were sure I'd wink at it? The pond,
thumbs tied, and . . . you know, Carter?
CARTER: Ay, I know.
But that won't hurt the girl.
SQUIRE: There's other girls
find London pleasanter than the fields—once there
she might be lost in London.
CARTER: What would you give
to have her in London willy-nilly?
SQUIRE: Much
to have her in London; more to know her safe
never to come from London—nor to leave
what cellar—or what deeper hole—she found.
CARTER: Umph. Well, for payment—
Leave me. You're too harsh
and if the old hag thinks to keep her house
she'll starve ere Rhoda cross the parish bounds.
Leave me. There's ways . . . and other ways . . . But
    the boy,
he won't stand still and see the lass thrown by.
SQUIRE: Damn him, if he must needs be young and gay,
hadn't London or Oxford or Bristol girls enough
that he must choose this hedge-flower? . . .
CARTER: If one night made one kind of fool of him,
mightn't another make a bigger kind?
As there's some folly in the blood that beats
so wholly natural.
SQUIRE: All his dreams mean this.
CARTER: No—this means all his dreams. I know the
    sort—
all shining fishlike scales of poetry
and shooting this way or the other through

an ocean of dark longing: there he goes,
sing hey! some colour or some food attracts
and there again he's off and deeper. Wait;
first the girl, then the old woman, last your son.
Where are they?

SQUIRE: All in there.

CARTER: I'll talk to them.
Go you to the house.

SQUIRE: That I should dread her blood
to warm themselves on the terrace in my sun!

[He goes out; and CARTER, going across, suddenly knocks and opens
the door. He steps back as DAN faces him]

CARTER: Hey now, what's this? it's never Dan come
    back?

DAN: You're a fine agent. Didn't you hear me come?
  Didn't you hear me stepping o'er the stiles?
  What else are agents for? Must not the rich
  have ears to listen lest a trespass shake
  the midnight dew from their thick grass or fright
  the wood-mice, which are valued being theirs?
  Master, the rich will look askance at you
  failing your duty.

CARTER: Ay, the same old Dan;
  you'd rather spend breath blowing at the lords
  than cool your own gruel with it. Blow your best.
  What shook in London—parliament or throne?
  or did you blow a coach down in the street?
  Why are you back, with some streets upright still?

DAN [angrily]: What's that to you, hired spy? you slink-
    ing prig,
  sneaking the crusts your masters leave the poor?
  I'd rather be a kerchief-snatching grab—

let be a gentleman of the road—than you,
fattened with dripping from your master's meat.
CARTER: Most like you will be.
DAN: Ah, and wait some days:
what if another rode on the squire's horse
who would not see her brother at a loss
for want of the agent's nag? You'd leg it then
over the stiles and far enough from here.

[RHODA, followed by GERALD, has come out of the cottage. She
     catches DAN's arm and speaks in his ear]

RHODA: Oaf, will you lose all?
DAN: Never fear, he's naught.
He's in the squire's hand and the squire in yours.
RHODA: And you in his and mine—either way lost
if one word slips to the runners. Fool, be quiet,
get to the wood and crouch there.
DAN: Look you, girl . . .
Well, but I only meant to fright him . . .
RHODA: Fright!
If he once let you fright him he'd be shamed
to see himself thereafter. Know your man
as I do, and can deal with him. Yes, now,
now even, I think I hold him. Off, you fool.

       [DAN mutters uneasily and then slips off

RHODA [calling after him]: You'll be in Bristol by to-
morrow night.
God bless you, brother.

   [CARTER strolls leisurely towards her, and glowers at GERALD]

CARTER: Bristol then, you think?
RHODA: Ay, he's a fancy for a ship.
CARTER: A ship!

I'd like to see your brother twisting ropes
some hundred feet above the waves, some ten
below the thunder.

RHODA: What can my mother do?
Here's the one man that's ours.

GERALD: Sweet, forbear
to think so meanly of the world; in me,
however poorly, all mankind is yours.

CARTER: Let me make my own offer, none the less,
discharging first your father's bidding. When
your leisure serves, he waits you at the house.
I've talked and he's grown calm.

GERALD: Calm's not enough.
Calm's to persuade him in. I will not sue;
he must intreat this lady—and my wife—
to find her lodging there.

CARTER: Well, give him time,
and take her pleasure first.

GERALD [taking RHODA aside]: Sweet, if he sends—
sends me—not then your lover but his son,
his name, his second self, his house—to pray
your courtesy to be his guest, your pride
would meet his so far graciously?

RHODA: O! yet
let me consider here a little while
what may be come on me. Dear, let me rest
and wonder what a most sweet madness wrought—

GERALD: But you must swear to love the madness still
for love's great sake that moved it. O princess,
you are the keystone of a mighty arch
wherein we all are builded—a new life,
a divine promise of diviner things.

RHODA: Alas, I see all things are shaken down
   about me and I cannot move ... I ... I ...
   Go now, I cannot think of things to say.
GERALD: You have no need to say things; you were made
   merely in your simplicity to be
   the meaning of all phrases. I will go,
   but promise me you will stay here at peace—
   peace which is all a silence, save it bear
   a bird's call as the promise of our love.
RHODA: I will remember. My dear lord, farewell.
GERALD: Farewell, until I come again in peace.
[*He goes out.* CARTER *has been watching from a little distance, and
                now comes down to* RHODA]
CARTER: Well, my girl?   [*She says nothing*]
                    Well? Come, Rhoda, not a word?
   Isn't this something sudden? If I dealt
   in promises and dreams and poetry
   and great Greek names the lad mouths out so well
   I should be peevish now.
RHODA: Ralph, I am shamed.
CARTER: Why no, not shamed; I never held you wise,
   being a woman—
RHODA: No, not wise; O Ralph—
   why did you make me other than myself?
CARTER: I make you other?
RHODA: It was nought to you—
   and I was nought—why did you threaten me
   with such a loftiness that all my strain
   could barely keep you from me, and my heart
   strained upward? It was that which ruined me,
   leaving me on my leftward side so bare
   that any thief could enter.

CARTER: And one did,
it seems; but not without your will.
RHODA: My will?
Dare you reproach me, when my will was numb,
under so strong a voice that beat it down,
I could not wrestle any more? Go now,
for you have lost now what you never gained
and he has lost what he could never gain,
and I have lost—O how much more than all
maidens who lose their maidenhood too soon!
CARTER: Women will have their choice and weep for it;
a woman needs must have a man to blame,
else she is ill at ease. Come now, my lass;
all's not lost yet, but you must pick your path
through the squire's fancies. He has whims and ways,
and your young lad there—a good fellow, true,
but something cock-a-hoop to beard the squire.
Don't lean on him too much.
RHODA: I will hear all
except to hear you say a word to me
that makes him other than a dream.
CARTER: A dream?
Gad, but you'll wake to worse than toothache. Tush,
don't talk so idly . . .Not but there's a truth
in what you say; these lads are fancy's dreams
to lasses of their age.
RHODA: Do not suppose
that I shall lean or turn or look for him,
whatever comes. I know what I have lost,
and I will stand up in the void; but you,—
Ralph, have some pity and go swiftly by.
CARTER: You make too much of this.

RHODA: I cannot make
too much of nothing, which is all I have.
CARTER: Why, if you've lost your stock in trade—
RHODA: O no,
my trade is all I have. It is my joy,
it is my terror, that is wholly gone.
CARTER: Your terror?
RHODA: My sweet fear, that was my strength.
Will you not go?
CARTER: Why, what's a boy to me?
RHODA: To think I hardly knew he kissed me!
CARTER: Faith,
there isn't much in poets making love,
a shadow kissing a shadow.
RHODA: No, not much;
only a shadow frightening a strong man.
CARTER: You need strength, don't you?
RHODA: I must find my own.
CARTER: You? yes, that's likely—you to be your strength.
Come, be advised, lass—
                [He takes hold of her arm]
RHODA: Ah, don't touch me! ah
I shall go mad with joy to feel you once
hold me—let go.
CARTER: Let go—for a boy's dream?
Are you a woman?
RHODA: No, I am nothing at all.
Loose me, and I shall know myself again.
CARTER: But if I will not?
RHODA: Hold me; let me die
here.
CARTER: You shall neither die nor go to him.

You are mine; you are mine; why did you wander, fool,
into a vapour?

RHODA: Ralph, I did not go—
you were not there and I was lost.

CARTER: By God,
I knew whose you must be . . . Enough. I'll see
the squire shall have his way and pay for all.
We will to London, we will—off, I say,
I must have time; the squire shall pay. . . .

ANNE [calling without]: Bess! Bess!

CARTER [hastily]: Play him a little—there's still time:
be kind to a dream, and we'll lose dreams.

[He goes out, and RHODA leans against the door of the hut in
exhaustion]

ANNE [entering]: Bess—Rhoda! Child, I've come for you.

RHODA: For me?

ANNE: Aye; Giles and I would have you sleep with us
at the farm—there's room.

RHODA: Sleep with you at the farm?

ANNE: Bless her, she's mazed. Why, you need friends, and
friends
may visit one another.

RHODA: Sleep with you?

ANNE: There, there. Is your mother in? I'll talk with her.
An end to all this witch's talk, and you
shall find the rest of us good fellows. Come,
I'll have my way, and we will all be friends.

RHODA: Friends?

ANNE: I'll go in. Bess!

[She goes into the hut

RHODA: Friends? Now, now to choose.
Aid me, my wit. If the squire fails, there's Ralph—

squire's daughter or the agent's mistress? One
I must trust somewhere. The boy's wife—and here?
Or London? Could I rise in London? Lords
and their gay houses? Trust me to slip Ralph
if a chance offers. Yet the other's safe
once reached—but there's much reaching; there's the
     squire.
Not Anne's bed anyhow—that's too far off
and too much guarded. London? but the risk
of him grown tired. Well, other girls than I
have lived in a king's palace. Gerald? Ralph?

                         [She goes into the hut

ACT III

[Three days later. RHODA and TESSA enter from the country]

TESSA: And there's the way the world wags. Well, it's
     good.
Keep pace with it, and chat, and be polite,
but never hold it necessary. No—
never want anything with all your heart,
although you work as if you did.

RHODA: But I—
can I . . .?

TESSA: As much as any. I've known girls
come from the country and be kept at court.
You're safe; I'm not. I trust my all on you—
that's if you come.

RHODA: If I were sure the squire
wouldn't give in . . .

TESSA: O lud, and if he does—
what do you gain? You'll be a country-wife,
only with men instead of pigs to feed.

Two weeks of this have tired me—forty years
I couldn't bear, nor you, child.
RHODA: Forty years!
TESSA: That's what you're fighting for; forty slow years
of sitting near to Gerald, reckoning gowns
and telling cooks how mutton should be dressed.
But O to see the link-boys in the Mall,
the coaches going to the House, the king
nodding to you perhaps—he did to me
summers ago.
RHODA: But what's in this for you
that you should help me, keep me, teach me what
to wear, and how to move—bring me by sly
paths to the privy-garden? That means gold—
why should you spend your gold on me?
TESSA: Why, thus:
it's a fair bargain, for a twelvemonth each.
I'm aging, but I'm not neglected; well,
I do not choose to cling, and be pushed down,
step by step, the back stairs, and end at last
among the link-boys and the horse-boys. No.
Let me step from the mistress to the friend;
I know the Duke's mood—you shall be my last
victorious battle. He will love me more
for bringing you and stepping back myself
than if I pestered him with thinning arms
and wrinkling cheeks. Practise a twelvemonth—then
for a twelvemonth after you have caught his ear,
you swear to serve me, whisper as I bid,
be zealous and be true. A twelvemonth, mark:
I ask no more—you may be true for that;
I wouldn't trust you longer.

RHODA: Do you think
such things could be?
TESSA: I know such things can be.
But you must answer now: this is the end—
I leave in an hour. I'm in the way down here;
if not, I'm in my own way. I had thought
that all was lost—till I saw you; but now
one triumph more—yours, yes, but yours for me.
RHODA: Won't the Duke wonder why you left town?
TESSA: You,
you, you, my answer: you for him—and me.
Well—choose. Choose for yourself. Remember, girl,
I don't so much love living as to beg
your help to aid me. If the bargain's good,
close it and come. If not, why, take your heir,
your agent, what you will. I drop you here
like the last card of a lost game—no more.
RHODA: I close, I close and come. But do not breathe
a word to any. I will slip away—
when?
TESSA: When the coach boy's whistle calls you. Soon,
an hour or less. It waits me, and I go.
RHODA: You'll keep your word?
TESSA: Child, I must keep my word
if you're to have a chance of breaking yours.
Listen, and join me at the cross-roads.
[She goes out towards the house
RHODA: Done.
Good-bye, my poet and my mother's game!
Good-bye, my Ralph and mine! Luck's in the cards,
and two must lose that two may win; and you,
mother, good-bye! and the corner in the hut

E

where I must shiver that the squire may itch,
and starve that farms may fear her. I can see
my fate as well as Malkin.

                                                  Malkin—pah!

                     [DAN slips in]
What are you doing here? have you gone mad
as well as mother—to come down by day?
DAN: What I want's money. You won't keep me there
tied to the trees, and any day forget
that I need food—and I know you, my lass—
you'd sell me to get favour with the squire.
RHODA: Half-a-dozen of you, but he wouldn't buy.
Get back, if you're wise; or stay here and get caught,
all's one—Ouf!

[With a magnificent stretch she throws off all the inconvenience of
                       her family]

DAN: To-day's rent day.
RHODA: Well, our rent
is a pint of hay-seed for the devil's chick
my mother's invisible imp she loves so well
she'd prick my blood out for his supper.
DAN: God,
you make me cold. I love warm fights—but this,
this dazes me.
RHODA: Yes, you're a coward at heart.
You fear the moon and our mother sitting lost
to all knowledge by the fire, and where she's gone
and what may come back with her, what new breath
be heard at nightfall, no face seen. I've sat
and heard the hut all shuffling with a crowd
of soft sly feet, and thickened pantings—beasts
pushing to get at mother by the fire,

and seen her giggle sideways, and then duck
curtsies to some one I could never see.
O and you roared in taverns, being brave!
DAN: If she's so clever can't she help?
RHODA: She is
so wise she never helps—except to help
harm some one, as to help me harms the squire.
I'm almost frightened still lest she should send
something to break an axle or to sit
behind the postboy and maliciously
fright him with songs of dead men's fingers twined
within his hair or something dodging him
just at the corner of his eye: not so
to bring me back, but rather turn the roads
all round the breaking coach into a maze
twisting for ever, and we never find
this hut or London or a thing but death.
DAN: My God,
can't you stop there? I don't want devil's tales
but honest things like gold. Rent day's to-day.
Where does the squire keep all his rent to-night?
and which way ride to-morrow when he goes
to take it down to Bristol?
RHODA: That's your guess—
not mine. Try asking him.
DAN: Can't you find out
from your gay lad?
RHODA: Why, Dan, you've a fresh mind.
If he come here to-night, and if I've time—
it's on his hour—I'd once grow sisterly,
for very joy of loosing. And you'd hang
quicker for that.

DAN: Ask, and let hanging chance
  as it may or may not if I get the gold.
RHODA: Get to that clump of trees—halfway 'twixt here
  and yonder cross-roads; if I hurry by
  and drop a word, catch it as you would catch
  the key of the Newgate cell you're sure to own.
DAN: If I could trust you—you can't do much harm.
  Does he come here each night?
RHODA: Each night; I yawn
  to music every evening, which he plays
  fingering my fingers like a lute . . He's here! [DAN goes
  Less than an hour, she said! O whistle, sound!
  Whistle me, London; there's a stalwart wench,
  London, is dying just for love of you.
  Here are kisses!
                    [CARTER comes in]
              Ralph!
CARTER: All's done.
RHODA: Done? what do you mean?
CARTER: All's ready, my lass. One thing about you girls
  that come undowered, there's no waiting round
  while you put finery on. To-night, to-night,
  this moment . . . there's a cart down by my house
  takes us some miles, then on to-morrow. Come.
  The squire was hard to part; his woman's gone,
  else he had waited longer—but he's paid.
RHODA: His woman's gone? what, gone?
CARTER: As good as gone;
  she was making for the coach; you'll see it soon
  go jolting by the cross roads. [He puts his arm round her
                    You and I
  go round the other way.

RHODA: O Ralph, so soon?

                              [She kisses him
but even poor girls have their hair to dress;
give me a moment—let me meet you there.
CARTER: No, no; we're one now. Your hair's trim enough;
come down to me and London, and farewell
to the squire's lambkin—or he'll be here too,
frisking about the common.
RHODA: One can slip,
better than two, away from him.
CARTER: But come
before he plays his gambols. Come, my girl.
RHODA: Well, just a moment. Let me have one look
at mother and the hut—only one look!
CARTER: What, you've grown whimsical? One look then,
    speed!
RHODA: And there's one thing. You know Dan's here?
CARTER: I know.
I don't guess why. I know he's slept three nights
in the wood since you cried 'Bless him' late when he
sought ship at Bristol.
RHODA: Mother won't let him go;
but truly now he's going. I came out
to bid him farewell—truly.
CARTER: There's no time.
One look, and off!

        [BESS comes to the door of the hut and sits down there
              Well done! now there's your look.
What more?
RHODA: Ralph, go down first. I'll come—one kiss,
She is my mother.
BESS: What, the serving-man?

Now isn't it a pity, serving-man,
you weren't born either poor or rich; there's wealth
and kingship either way, or here or there,
in soft sheets, or in none. But you run waste
between them, all you cosy middle men!
Porters and panders—that's your work.
CARTER: One look—
haven't you had it?
BESS: One look—yes, that's yours,
at the ankles, under your eyelids, when the coach
stops, and your better's lady mounts the steps,
and you make jokes in the kitchen as a sop
for the hungry beast that rends you.
CARTER   Rhoda!
RHODA: Aye,
I'm coming. Only a moment. Let me alone
to nuzzle her a moment.
CARTER: Not a tick.
Will you have me carry you?
                    [GERALD comes in]
RHODA: Gerald!
CARTER: That's fine;
let's have the parish up to shout good-bye.
GERALD: I am permitted, fairest? I have watched,
I think, a change of seasons, not of hours,
since we dislinked. To-night's a golden night
and makes amends. Come, we will watch the star
that brought me to you: 'Hesperus, that led
the starry host'—O Rhoda, you must learn
the supreme language. Milton will not be
Milton until I hear him from your lips.
All the great poets, I know now, lacked this,

your voice to make them what they meant to be;
even Shelley, even Shakespeare. I await the hour
when on our terrace you, with that sole voice,
the only sweeter thing than that you read,
shall sound about me as the sun's light flows
now, in a feeble prophecy of you.
Good-evening, Bess.
BESS: Good-evening, gentleness.
Gentleness or gentility or both?
GERALD: Both, if it may be. I would have them one,
and will you tell me that they cannot be?
BESS: Ah! but gentility always gets his will
out of poor gentleness. Which you will be
to Rhoda yonder makes you the other one
to that great man the squire your father.
GERALD: Bess,
believe that I am gentleness to her
and valour for her. I have talked with him;
all works for the best. He's hasty but he's good.
BESS: Good? what's good? wanting a thing not quite
    enough
to make yourself uneasy for it. Bad?
bad's wanting a thing so much that all yourself
is a small price to pay; but there's a third
tribe, that is neither good nor bad, possessed
by something not themselves and beyond earth,
coming to earth through holes—and they the holes;—
that's why your father, when he runs in hell,
down the low, smoky, greasy corridors,
under the roof he knocks his skull against,
will whimper while I sit upon his neck,
scratching his shoulders with sharp claws; for I

grow daily to need nothing but my lord
the black, but he wails out for house and lands.
GERALD: Speak lightly of him; he's my father, Bess.
CARTER [to RHODA]: Now, while he's talking, slip away
    with me.
RHODA [seeing a hope of distraction]:
   With you? why, Gerald!
GERALD: Princess?
RHODA: Must your man
invite me into corners? where's the need
he and I should be intimate?
BESS: la la!
Porter or pander, your job's done; the gate
swung open. You're paid, porter: pander, go.
GERALD: Carter, you wanted me?
CARTER: Not you, not you.
   Rhoda!
GERALD: Halt there. My father is of blood,
and may be pardoned if he speaks in rage;
his hired man has no place with queens.
BESS: O hey!
See how he jumps, the chickling; here and there
now on one's shoulder, now on t'other's. Mark
that curvet backward! there's a somersault
in mid-air over their heads. Now, my young squire,
he's pulling your hair.
CARTER: See here, I do not mean—
GERALD: My lady will excuse your going.
RHODA: Yes,
with all my heart and never heart so glad.
BESS: O yes, one other. I am gladder than you,
daughter, to see the discharged footman sprawl

at foot of the steps, for my black master and I
hate the poor fools whose thirst must needs be quenched
by heel-taps.

CARTER: God, there's but one heel-tap here.

[RHODA screams. ANNE comes in]

ANNE: Good-evening, Master Gerald. Good-evening, all.

GERALD: Good-evening, Anne.

BESS: Good-evening, gracious Anne.

[There is a moment of entire silence]

ANNE: I hope I'm not come awkwardly?

BESS [half-aside to her]: In time.
The agent there is having words with the squire,
that's the young squire. Such words. It shouldn't be;
you've a kind heart, speak to them, patch a peace:
O Anne, how nice to have God help you so.
There's few things that I better love to see
than a quarrel settled by a woman's wit.

GERALD [before ANNE can get near]: Carter, I can't have
heard you.

CARTER: Let me speak
one word apart with her.

RHODA: No, Gerald, no.
Look, I won't stop here now. Do you two find
each other's meaning. I will walk as far
as the cross-roads—and you'll be better friends.

GERALD: Do not go, Rhoda. Won't you speak with him?

RHODA: No. Let me go.

GERALD: It were foul shame, my sweet,
upon these fields to give another place,
for you are the first lady of our house—
the first and only, since my mother died.
Carter, we will withdraw.

CARTER: I'll not withdraw.
Learn manners, my fine Oxford boy. This girl
promised to come with me to London; now
I only ask her why she's changed her mind.
I don't even knock her down.
GERALD: You're merely mad.
Rhoda—to London? and with you? You're mad.
BESS: A dozen Malkins—all as spry as spry
legging it with the best into their mouths
and out again! Did you see that larger one
twitching the stick in his hand? that little mite
pinching the young squire's ear? O Anne, be quick.
Don't let them start to kill each other, Anne.
ANNE: I think you've all gone mad. Excuse me, Sir,
I came up here to have a word with Bess,
a little earlier than I use—that's why
you and I meet here—two men asked the way
up through the wood—two Bow Street men.
BESS: Boy Dan!
scramble, my lad!
CARTER: Hey, there's your brother gone,
my lady squiress. He'll hang here in chains,
fine sight from your new bedroom!
GERALD: As God lives,
you shall be silent.

[A whistle sounds, as DAN rushes in. CARTER turns to meet him.
RHODA makes a movement to rush past him, but GERALD catches
her and holds her back]

GERALD: Rhoda, stay: is it he they want?
RHODA: O God,
do I care? let go!
GERALD: Hold back! you'll get some hurt.

CARTER: What, all the family here?
She suits her brother; that's true, too. You stop,
as she stops, so she says. No, not this way.

[There is a moment of utter silence, and the whistle at a distance
    sounds again]

RHODA: Off, off, you fool!

[She flings GERALD away from her, and he reels between DAN and
    CARTER as the latter strikes at DAN with his stick. The blow hits
    GERALD's head and he falls. CARTER springs back, and DAN
    taking advantage of the movement rushes forward and disappears
    on the opposite side. Silence follows again, broken by a single
    loud hoot of delight from BESS: RHODA has hurried away]

CARTER: Gerald!
ANNE [running across]: You've hurt him. [She kneels down
                            He's . . . he's stunned.
BESS: Dead, dead!
I knew it! O I saw it! O who sat,
light as a feather on the cudgel's top
weighting it himward? O squire, squire! Now buzz,
my precious Malkin, buzz him, sting him here! . . .
There's water in the hut, Anne.   [She sees CARTER's stick
                            O blood, blood!
Ah hoo! ah hoo! His ghost'll hang in the hut
beside his father's twitching baby wish;
blood, blood, ah hoo!
ANNE: For God's sake, Bess!
BESS: He's dead?
Too late for peace, good woman? . . .what . . . what
    . . . O!
Delicate game! Anne, you're too late for peace,
but not for justice.

ANNE [standing up: CARTER is still busy with the body]:
     Justice?

BESS: You were here;
Anne, it's your duty. They won't take my word,
but when a man has killed he ought to swing.
Didn't you hear the pretty agent swear
that he'd have vengeance? Look what vengeance
   does!

ANNE: No, surely he didn't mean it—

BESS: Surely he did;
ah Anne, you're too good; you don't understand
how a man strikes. But still you heard? you heard?
You mustn't tell a lie now, must you, Anne?

ANNE: I heard them quarrelling—but what they said
to a word or two—

BESS: Poor Gerald! Anne, be just;
you mustn't be too kind. Gerald must have
justice, although he's dead. Remember, Anne,
murdered men's ghosts haunt all those who forbid
death for death, hate for hate, and blood for blood.

ANNE: Where's Rhoda?   [She looks round

BESS: Rhoda? somewhere round.

ANNE: Who's that?
Bess, Bess, that's Rhoda!

BESS [staring after her]:   That's Rhoda? yes, it is.
A coach for Rhoda, too! now if she's gone—

[The SQUIRE comes in, seeing CARTER. The two women are a little
               out of the way]

SQUIRE: Carter, he's caught!

CARTER [staring round]:   He's caught!

SQUIRE: Yes, Dan from here.

Have you caught the girl?   [He sees GERALD's body
                    What's that?   That's Gerald.
BESS [looking round]   Squire!
SQUIRE: That's Gerald! O my God . . .!
CARTER [after a moment]   There's been a bit
of a scuffle. I hit at Dan . . .
BESS: Are you sure of that?
CARTER: Dan slipped the Bow Street runners and nigh got
clear off . . .
ANNE: Chut, Mr. Carter! better keep quiet!
BESS: Dear
sweet Anne, he can't keep quiet: hell aches in him
when he can't use his tongue. He is his tongue.
Now I am almost happy. Speak, my squire,
I am nigh happy; speak, and perfect it.
SQUIRE: Who did this?
                    Who did this?
                                Will none of you
speak? Who did this?
CARTER: Well, in a way, I did . . .
an accident . . . a . . . a . . . I'm sorry, squire.
BESS: He's sorry, squire. But I'm not sorry, squire.
He did it.
CARTER: Jailbird's mother, hold your tongue.
ANNE: Sh! Sh! it's a bad business.
SQUIRE: You did this?
CARTER: In a way.
SQUIRE: You did this? What have I done to you
that you should twist my life out of its case?
CARTER: I wouldn't hurt you . . . I was angry, yes,
but not to strike him . . . not to—
SQUIRE: There's cold air

all round me; there's a bleak wind somewhere. Who
told you which way he threw his arm at night
when he was little? Did you strike him so
that he should fall so? Do you feel the wind?
It means death—Gerald's dead, and yet it blows.
You'll die; you'll hang for this.

CARTER: No, I shan't hang.

SQUIRE [looking at ANNE]: Why did he do it?

BESS: Now, Anne, justice first.

ANNE: Squire, there were quarrels—what about God
knows—
but hot words and . . . and . . . somehow . . .

BESS [intensely in ANNE's ear]: Anne, you know.
[slowly] You know you heard him promise vengeance.
Speak.

ANNE: And . . . somehow . . . I heard something said . . .
no, no,
he didn't mean it . . . vengeance . . . I don't know.

SQUIRE: Vengeance? [with a roar] Aye, vengeance. Hunt
him down! Ah! Ah!

[CARTER turns and runs

BESS: Stand still, my squire! stand still.

SQUIRE: You?

BESS: Now all's done
You're empty and I'm full. Now your boy's gone
and only little goblins walk the house
and sit with you at supper, and a Death
on the other side the table. Centuries since
did you not tell me that my son was caught?
Aye, did you add my daughter's run away?
She has, to London. Now at last I'm free.
Now there's not any creature in the world

to hold me in; now I am all at ease
to grin and squat with Malkin. But you're down;
let your walls run o'er all the common, Death
rides them astride and always drives them back,
till they close in and crush you. You need hands
to clasp yours, and there won't be any, squire!
Ohoo! Ohoo!

         [The SQUIRE stares at her imbecilely and goes out

ANNE: Bess, you should let him be.
It isn't his fault Rhoda . . .

BESS: Anne, my chuck,
if aught were his fault I should hate him less.
His fault no more than yours, and when he's dead,
and my poor wandering hate gets free again
I shouldn't wonder if it came and sat
over against your farm-door. Look for it, Anne;
you'll know it by its pointed shining snout—
you'll see it best in the dark; or since you're dull
mayhap your baby'll see it. Ask it, Anne,
ask it each evening what was hiding there
in the gutter under the wall.   [ANNE goes out
                    And all you else,
comfortable pleasant people through the world,
you who sit close by fires or train your flowers
in gardens, as the wind blows; you who talk
most of your neighbours' doings, all you fair
lasses and jingling-penny boys, and plump
matrons, a thing goes wandering o'er the earth
you cannot see, a thing that dark or day
are all alike to, burrowing through all walls,
that is madness, and is sickness, and is hate,
and is a marvellous thing beyond all these—

being that which first God saw when he beheld
pure evil. Into your houses and your breasts,
till you shall wither and look all awry
with twisted faces, it shall slide along;
farewell, fair lasses; farewell, gallant boys;
farewell, you comfortable folk, farewell,
but this shall be among you till you die.

Milton Keynes UK
Ingram Content Group UK Ltd.
UKHW041844121024
449535UK00004B/318

9 781528 708722